This Book Belongs To:

Bright

Sparks

Thank you for buying this Bright Sparks book.

We donate one book to less fortunate children for every two sold.
We have already donated over 150,000 books.

We want to help the world to read.

This is a Bright Sparks book
This edition published in 2002
Bright Sparks, Queen Street House,
4 Queen Street, BATH BA1 1HE, UK
Copyright © Parragon 2001

this book was created by
small world creations ltd

Printed in China.
ISBN 1-84250-524-6

Benny the Barmy Builder

Bright ☆ Sparks

Benny was a hard-working builder, but sometimes he could be forgetful! One morning, Benny the Builder arrived bright and early at Vet Vicky's surgery.

"Benny the Builder at your service!" he announced.
"I think you have a job for me to do."

"Not today, Benny," replied Vicky. "But Polly Postlady is expecting you!"
"Of course!" said Benny. "I really shouldn't be so forgetful!"
And off he went to Polly the Postlady's house.

"Benny the Builder at your service!" Benny announced.
"**Woof!**" barked Benny's dog, Rocky.

Polly took out a drawing to show Benny.
"I want you to build a play house in my garden," Polly said.
"It's a surprise for my grandchildren, Peter, Penny and Patty."

Benny and Polly looked at the drawing together.

"The play house should have two doors," said Polly,
"one at the front and one at the back."

"Yes, I see,"
said Benny.

"There should be five windows," said Polly,
"one at either side of the front door and
one on each of the the other sides."

"Yes, I see," said Benny.
"And I want a nice sloping roof," said Polly, "not a flat roof!"

Polly left for the post office, and Benny went out to start work. But he had barely begun when a gust of wind came along.

WHOOSH! went Polly's drawing, up in the air.

"WOOF!" barked Rocky, leaping up to catch it.

Oh no!

The drawing got caught in the branches of a tree!

Rocky fetched the drawing but by the time
Benny got it back, it was in shreds.

"Oh dear!" moaned Benny the Builder.
"How will I build the play house now?"

Benny tried to remember
everything in the drawing.
But he quickly got very confused!

"Was it five windows and two
doors?" Benny puzzled.

"Or was it two windows and five doors?

"Was the roof flat and not sloping? Or sloping and not flat?

"Oh dear, Oh dear!"

Benny decided that he would just have to do the best he could.

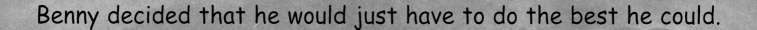

He got to work measuring...
mixing...laying bricks...

...sawing wood...
hammering nails...

...fixing screws plastering and painting...

...and doing his very best to make everything just right.

Late that afternoon, Postlady Polly got home from work.

She couldn't wait to see what Benny had done.

But, what a **surprise** she had!

The play house's roof was flat. The bottom of the house was sloping. There were two doors on one side of the house.

There were two floors, both different sizes.
And there were two windows on one side of the house.

"It's all wrong!" said Polly. "How will you ever fix it in time?"

Benny didn't have a chance to answer, because just then,
Polly's grandchildren arrived.

"Look! A play house!"
they cried happily, rushing towards it.

"There's a door for each of us!" they all cried together.
"And we can climb right up to the roof!" said Patty.

"And slide down the other side!" said Peter.
"And there are loads of windows so it's nice and bright inside!" said Penny.

"Granny, it's the **best** play house ever!" the children told Polly.
"Thank you so much!"

"Well, I think you should thank Benny the Builder," said Postlady Polly.

Benny the Builder smiled too. "I just did my very best," he said.